Daniel's First Sleepover

adapted by Angela C. Santomero

based on the screenplay "Daniel's Sleepover" written by Becky Friedman

poses and layouts by Jason Fruchter

Simon Spotlight

New York   London   Toronto   Sydney   New Delhi

SIMON SPOTLIGHT
An imprint of Simon & Schuster Children's Publishing Division
1230 Avenue of the Americas, New York, New York 10020
First Simon Spotlight paperback edition January 2015
© 2015 The Fred Rogers Company
All rights reserved, including the right of reproduction in whole or in part in any form.
SIMON SPOTLIGHT and colophon are registered trademarks of Simon & Schuster, Inc.
For information about special discounts for bulk purchases, please contact Simon & Schuster
Special Sales at 1-866-506-1949 or business@simonandschuster.com.
Manufactured in the United States of America 1214 LAK
10 9 8 7 6 5 4 3 2 1
ISBN 978-1-4814-2893-4 (pbk)
ISBN 978-1-4814-2894-1 (eBook)

It's nighttime in the Neighborhood of Make-Believe. Daniel Tiger is wearing his pajamas. But he's not going to bed just yet. . . .

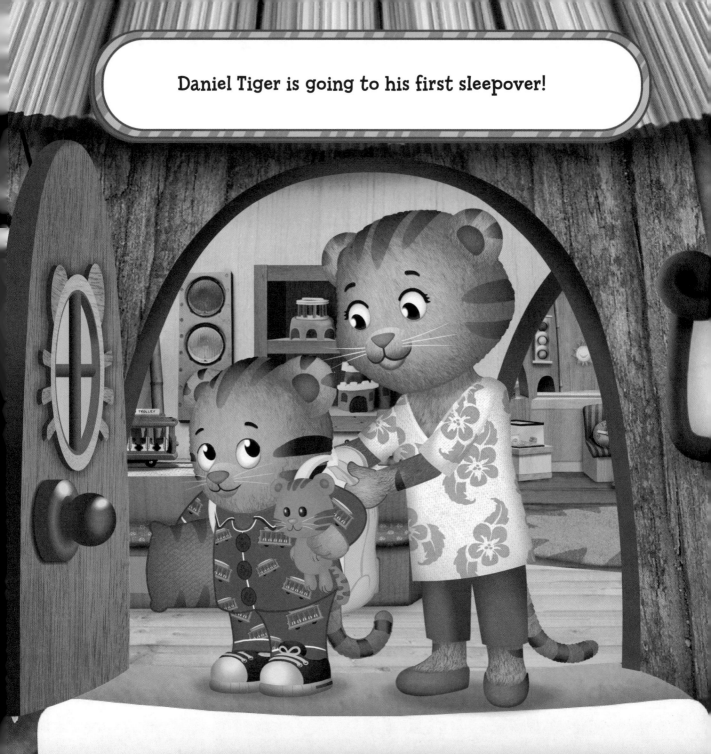

Daniel Tiger is going to his first sleepover!

Daniel is so excited. He hops on Trolley and says, "Trolley, please take us to Prince Wednesday's castle."

Daniel and Mom sing, "*We're going to the castle for a royal sleepover! Won't you ride along with me? Ride along! Won't you ride along with me?*"

Daniel is not sure what he's going to do at the sleepover.
He sings, *"When we do something new, let's talk about what we'll do."*
Then Daniel asks Mom, "What will I do at the sleepover?"

Mom says, "You will do everything you do before going to bed at home. But you get to do it all with Prince Wednesday!" That sounds exciting to Daniel as he remembers all of the things he does before going to bed. Daniel brushes his teeth, reads a story, and sings a song.

Prince Wednesday is waiting for Daniel in his bedroom. "A royal hello to you!" says Prince Wednesday. "Boop-she-boop-she-boo! And to YOU too, neighbor!"

Daniel notices that they are both wearing their pajamas. Daniel has never worn his pajamas to someone else's house before! Daniel giggles and says, "Do you want to make believe with me? Let's make believe that we're having a pajama dance party!"

Daniel imagines that they are at a pajama dance party. All of Prince Wednesday's stuffed animals join the party too.

A pajama dance party is so much fun.
We dance and play until the day is done.
Dancing in your pj's is oh so sweet.
We dance with our hands and we dance with our feet!
At a pajama party, we play at night.
And when the fun is done, we snuggle up and sleep tight!

"Wasn't that grr-ific?" says Daniel. Daniel and Prince Wednesday are getting sleepy. It's dark outside in the Neighborhood of Make-Believe, and even the birds are going to sleep.

It's time for Prince Wednesday and Daniel to get ready for bed.

With lots of giggles and bubbles, Prince Wednesday and Daniel brush their teeth.

They even sing the same song when they brush their teeth!

"*I gotta brusha brusha brusha brush my teeth at night, if I wanna keep them healthy and bright. I gotta brusha brusha brusha brush my teeth.*" Brushing teeth together is something that makes sleepovers different and fun.

Now it's time for Daniel and Prince Wednesday to snuggle in bed to hear a bedtime story. They get cozy with lots of stuffed animal friends. Being together makes sleepovers different and fun!

King Friday reads the boys their favorite book, *Tigey, the Adventure Tiger*. King Friday is royally funny as he reads in all of the jungle animals' voices. The boys laugh and laugh.

Now it's time for a bedtime song. Daniel sings goodnight to Prince Wednesday. Prince Wednesday takes off his glasses and sings goodnight back to Daniel. Sleepovers make bedtime different and fun. Daniel smiles.

Now it's time to turn out the light and go to sleep. But wait!

There is a great big shadow on the wall. It looks scary to Daniel! What could it be? Daniel remembers, if something seems scary, "See what it is. You might feel better."

The boys hop out of bed and investigate the great big shadow. What is it?

It's just Mr. Lizard! Mr. Lizard is not scary. Mr. Lizard is not scary at all!

Daniel hugs Mr. Lizard and crawls back into bed next to Prince Wednesday. Now they can go to sleep, together, at their very first sleepover.

Goodnight, Daniel. Goodnight, Prince Wednesday. And goodnight, neighbor. Ugga Mugga!